WITHDRAWN

Dory Story

by
Jerry Pallotta

Illustrated by
David Biedrzycki

 Charlesbridge

My mom and dad always told me, "You're just a kid, so don't ever go out in the boat alone!"

But one night I learned about plankton. These tiny sea creatures are invisible during the day, but sometimes, after dark, they light up.

I wanted to learn more.

he next morning the ocean was flat calm.

I couldn't resist!

I pushed the dory out and decided to row to the big rock in the middle of the bay.

As I rowed,
I noticed dozens of
seabirds circling around.

Grandpa says
that where there are
seabirds there are fish,
so I kept on rowing.

**I** looked over the side of the boat.

I saw hundreds and hundreds of tiny shrimp swimming.

I guessed that
the little shrimp
were eating
the plankton.

**A**s I rowed
toward the big rock,
I saw schools of sand lances.

Some people call
these fish sand eels.

The sand eels were chasing
and eating the shrimp.

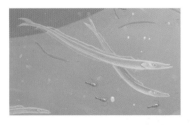

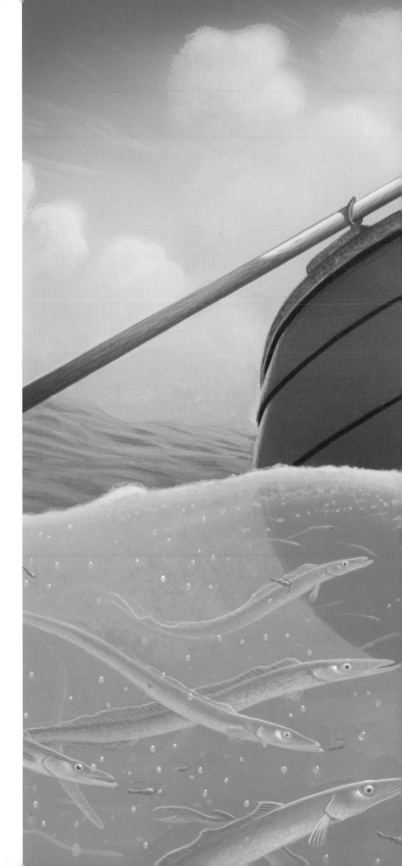

 heard something splash,
and I looked over the bow of the boat.

I heard more splashes.

I looked closer and saw mackerels
chasing and eating the sand eels.

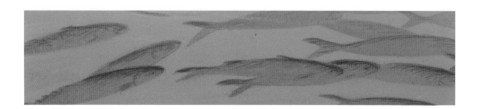

hen I saw them. Bluefish!
Yikes! The bluefish were swimming
like crazy and eating the mackerels.
It was a feeding frenzy.

Bluefish have razor-sharp teeth.
I learned that the hard way. Last year
I put my fingers into the mouth of a
bluefish to pull my hook out—zap!
I had to get four stitches.

**I** stood up in the dory to watch the show the bluefish were putting on.

Suddenly five huge tuna appeared in the bay!

The tuna were chasing and eating the bluefish.

I began to worry.
Maybe going out
in the boat alone
wasn't such a
good idea.

The tuna were
almost as long
as the boat.

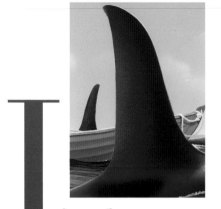

I've been scared a few times, but I was terrified when killer whales came into the bay chasing the tuna. I didn't know what to do.

But it all started to make sense. Killer whales eat tuna, tuna eat bluefish, bluefish eat mackerels, mackerels eat sand eels, sand eels eat shrimp, and shrimp eat plankton.

I knew one thing—I didn't want to become part of the food chain. Help! Where's my mommy?

Just as I decided to
row back to shore, whammo!
A humungous humpback whale
breached right in front of me.

But wait—humpback whales
don't eat killer whales.
Humpbacks eat plankton
and krill, some of the tiniest
creatures in the ocean.
The food chain is really
more like a food web.

 should have been
smart like the seals
and stayed near shore.

The harbor seals had
sensed the danger and
pulled themselves out
of the water to escape
the killer whales.

**A**ll of a sudden
a killer whale swam
by, chasing a tuna.

The tuna jumped out
of the water and smashed
into my dory. Bam!

Oh, no! I was capsized.
Thank God I had my
life jacket on.

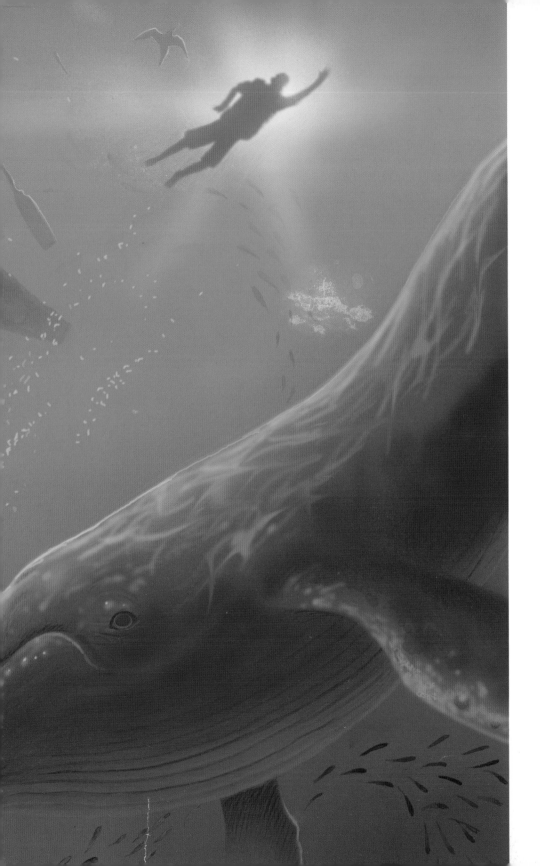

 should have stayed with the boat to wait for help, but I was scared, and I started swimming.

I swam through the shrimp, the eels, the mackerels, the bluefish, the tuna, the killer whales, and the humpback whale. It was cold. I had water in my nose, but I kept swimming toward that rock in the middle of the bay.

I made it!

I pulled myself up
by grabbing onto the seaweed.

Just then,
I heard my mom's voice. . . .

"Danny, you tell the best stories when you're in the bathtub! You should write a book."

2004 first paperback edition

Text copyright © 2000 by Jerry Pallotta

Illustrations copyright © 2000 by David Biedrzycki

Published by Charlesbridge

85 Main Street, Watertown, MA 02472

(617) 926-0329

www.charlesbridge.com

Library of Congress Cataloging-in-Publication Data

Pallotta, Jerry.

    Dory story/Jerry Pallotta; illustrated by David Biedrzycki.

        p.   cm.

    Summary: While taking a bath with his new red toy dory,
a boy imagines himself alone on the ocean getting a first-hand look
at the ocean's food chain.

    ISBN 978-0-88106-075-1 (reinforced for library use)

    ISBN 978-0-88106-076-8 (softcover)

    ISBN 978-1-60734-196-3 (ebook pdf)

    [1. Boats and boating—Fiction. 2. Marine animals—Fiction.
3. Marine plants—Fiction. 4. Ocean—Fiction. 5. Baths—Fiction.]
I. Biedrzycki, David, ill. II. Title.

PZ7.P1785Do   1999

[E]—dc21   98-37756

Printed by Sung In Printing
in Gunpo-Si, Kyonggi-Do, Korea

(hc) 15 14 13 12 11

(sc) 15 14 13 12

The illustrations in this book were done in acrylic on
Strathmore illustration board.

Designed by Bob Biedrzycki

Zillion

Thank you, Mom and Dad, for buying me a toy dory when
I was five years old and a real dory when I was fourteen!
— Jerry Pallotta

To my brother, Bob, who taught me how to draw
(The little "c" inside the big "C")
— David Biedrzycki